Little Tiger, Get Well Soon!

Janosch

Little Tiger,
Get Well Soon!

*The tale of Little Tiger
when he was feeling ill*

Translated by Anthea Bell

Scholastic Publications Limited
London

Scholastic Publications Ltd.,
10 Earlham Street, London WC2H 9RX, UK

Scholastic Inc.,
730 Broadway, New York, NY 10003, USA

Scholastic Tab Publications Ltd.,
123 Newkirk Road, Richmond Hill,
Ontario L4C 3G5, Canada

Ashton Scholastic Pty. Ltd.,
P O Box 579, Gosford, New South Wales,
Australia

Ashton Scholastic Ltd.,
165 Marua Road, Panmure, Auckland 6,
New Zealand

First published in Switzerland by Diogenes Verlag AG Zürich, 1985
under the title *Ich mach dich gesund, sagte der Bär*.
First published in the UK by Andersen Press Ltd., 1986

Published in paperback by Scholastic Publications Ltd., 1988

Copyright © Diogenes Verlag AG Zürich, 1985
This translation copyright © Andersen Press Ltd., 1986

ISBN 0 590 70797 3

All rights reserved

Made and printed in Hong Kong

One day Little Tiger came out of the
wood, hobbling.
He couldn't walk properly.
He couldn't stand properly.
He fell over and lay there, just where he was,
on the ground in the middle of the meadow.

Little Bear came running up at once. 'What's the matter, Tiger?' he cried. 'Are you ill?'

'Yes,' said Little Tiger. 'I'm terribly ill. I can hardly move.'

'Well, never mind,' said Little Bear. *'I will make you better.'*

Little Tiger had not picked any mushrooms, he had not written Little Bear a letter while he was out, he hadn't even been pulling his stripy tiger duck along.

'Whereabouts does it hurt?' asked Little Bear. 'Show me!'

'Here,' said Little Tiger, pointing first to one paw and then to the other. 'And here! And my legs hurt too, and I hurt in front and behind, and on my left and on my right, and on top and down below.'

'You mean you hurt all over?' said
Little Bear. 'Then I'll have to carry
you.'

And he started to carry Little Tiger
home.

'You must bandage me up too,'
Little Tiger told him.

'Yes, of course,' said Little Bear.

So once they were home, he put Little Tiger down on the table, just as if they were really at the doctor's.

'My paw first,' said Little Tiger.

So Little Bear bandaged up his paw.

The *first* paw.

Then he bandaged up the other paw.

'Now my legs,' said Little Tiger.

So Little Bear bandaged up his legs.

'Where else?' he asked.

'My back,' said Little Tiger.

But if you are bandaging somebody's back you have to bandage his chest as well.

So Little Bear wound the bandage round and round Little Tiger's back and chest. And as there was plenty of bandage left he bandaged Little Tiger all over, from top to toe.

'Leave my head out,' said Little Tiger.

'I might want to cough.'

By the time Little Tiger was all bandaged up he was feeling rather better. But then he felt rather worse again, because he was hungry.

'I'll cook you something nice to eat,' said Little Bear. 'Tell me your favourite food!'

'River trout with almond sauce, new potatoes and breadcrumbs.'

'There isn't any of that,' said Little Bear. 'Try something else.'

'Egg noodles with almond sauce and breadcrumbs,' said Little Tiger.

'There isn't any of that either,' said Little Bear. 'Try another something else.'

'Breadcrumbs,' said Little Tiger.

But there weren't any breadcrumbs either.

'Try saying *soup*,' said Little Bear.

'Oh yes, *soup*,' cried Little Tiger. 'Just
what I was going to say myself.'

'And little raspberries out of the garden
for pudding,' said Little Bear.

So he made Little Tiger some delicious
soup, with potatoes and carrots out of the
garden, and he put some parsley in it,

and there were a few shiny little beads of fat floating on top, and when Little Tiger had drunk it he began to feel rather better.

But then he began to feel rather worse again, because he wanted to settle down and go to sleep.

'Go to bed,' said Little Bear.

'No, I want to sleep on our nice plushy sofa with its soft cushions,' said Little Tiger, 'all tucked up in the spotty leopard rug.'

So Little Bear put Little Tiger on the nice plushy sofa with its soft cushions, and tucked him up in the spotty leopard rug.

And Little Tiger slept for a while.

When he woke up, he was feeling rather better.

But then he began to feel rather worse again, because he wanted visitors.

Little Bear went into the garden, picked
up the garden hose, and rang Auntie Goose
on the underground telephone line, by way
of the moles' telephone exchange.

'Hullo, who's speaking?' he asked. 'Is that Auntie Goose?'

'Yes, Auntie Goose here. I can hear you loud and clear. Who is it calling, please?'

'It's me. Little Bear speaking! Tiger is ill, but he's going to get well soon.'

'Which Tiger would that be?' asked Auntie Goose.

'*Our* Tiger, of course!' said Little Bear.
'Oh,' said Auntie Goose, 'then I'll come
round straight away!'
    And before you could say Jack Robinson
. . .

there was Auntie Goose on the doorstep.

She had flown part of the way across the fields, and then she had swum the river, and she had waddled the last part of the way on foot, from the river to the house.

'I've brought him some gooseberry cordial,' said Auntie Goose. 'It cures everything. Well, at least it never hurt anyone yet.'

When Little Tiger had drunk a small glass of gooseberry cordial he began to feel rather better.

But then he felt rather worse again, because he wanted more visitors.

The hare with the fast running shoes
came calling.

'I hear Little Tiger's ill,' he said. 'The
mole told me.

What's the matter with him, then?'

'What's the matter with you, then, Tiger?' asked Little Bear.

'I don't know,' said Little Tiger.

'We don't know,' said Little Bear.

'Then he'll have to be examined,' said the hare with the fast running shoes.

'Then you'll have to be examined, Tiger,' said Little Bear.

'By Doctor Bullfrog,' said the hare with the fast running shoes.

'By Doctor Bullfrog, Tiger,' said Little Bear.

'At the Animals' Hospital,' said the hare with the fast running shoes.

'At the Animals' Hospital, Tiger,' said Little Bear.

'Tomorrow?' asked Little Tiger.

'Tomorrow,' said Little Bear and the hare with the fast running shoes and Auntie Goose.

So then Little Tiger felt rather better again, because it is nice at the Animals' Hospital.

Little Bear slept on the sofa with Little Tiger that night, to help him get better.

And next day Little Tiger really was
feeling rather better, and his bandages
came off.

But then he felt rather worse again, because he wanted to go to the Animals' Hospital.

Along came the big strong wolf and a big strong billygoat with a stretcher, because if you are ill you have to be carried on a stretcher.

'You will be careful, won't you?' said Little Bear. 'Pick Tiger up carefully and mind you don't drop him, because he's my friend.'

But then Little Bear decided to pick Tiger up himself.

They wanted to take the spotty leopard rug as well, so Auntie Goose went inside to fetch it.

They hadn't gone far when they met the great big, kind grey elephant.

'Where are you people going, then?' asked the elephant.

'To the Animals' Hospital,' said Little Bear. 'Tiger's ill, and we're making him better.'

'Then I'll go part of the way with you,' said the great big, kind grey elephant. 'I might come in useful.'

Then they met the yellow duck, and the
hare who lived in the wood, and they met a
mouse, a fox, the dog, the hedgehog, and the
wandering donkey with a rucksack on his
back, and all those animals went along too.

'Is it much farther?' asked Little Tiger.

'Almost exactly eight hundred metres. As the crow flies,' said the big strong wolf. 'Look, you can see it now!'

'Where?' asked Little Tiger.

'Down there,' said the big strong wolf.

'I can't see a thing,' said Little Tiger.

'Farther over to the left,' said the big strong wolf, and then Little Tiger could see it too.

So that was all right.

'Do mind you don't drop Little Tiger!' said Little Bear. 'You know he's ill!'

They carried him very, very carefully into the Animals' Hospital.

First they went through the big doors, then they went down a long corridor.

'Ward Number Five,' said Nurse Lucy. Nurse Lucy was very nice. She was a real duck.

The fox was in Ward Number Five too. He had broken his paw.

He said he had been in a fight with the lion, and he claimed to have won.

But that was all lies. He had got his paw jammed in the henhouse door when he was trying to steal chickens.

So now he was in hospital, with his broken paw in plaster, and serve him right.

'When you come into hospital you get a clean nightshirt to wear,' said Nurse Lucy.

Little Tiger tried his nightshirt on. It was a perfect fit.

'And then you get a bath,' said Nurse
Lucy, 'to make you smell nice and clean.'
'Here, Tiger,' said Little Bear, 'try this
lovely sweet-smelling rose-petal soap.'

Then it was time for Little Tiger to be examined.

'Take a deep breath,' said Doctor Bullfrog.

'Ooh,' went Little Tiger.

'Deeper than that,' said Doctor Bullfrog.

'Oooooh,' went Little Tiger.

'Even deeper,' said Doctor Bullfrog.

'Ooooooooooooooh.'

'Excellent,' said Doctor Bullfrog, and he listened to Little Tiger. First he listened to the front of him, then he listened to the back of him, and then the examination was over.

'I prescribe Mr Tiger his favourite food three times a day,' said Doctor Bullfrog. 'And his favourite pudding to follow. What do you like to eat best, Mr Tiger?'

'River trout with almond sauce and breadcrumbs!' cried Little Tiger.

'That will do nicely,' said Doctor Bullfrog.
'And of course I prescribe the same for Little
Bear as well.'

Little Tiger began to feel rather better
again at once.

The next examination was an X-ray.

'What's an X-ray?' asked Little Bear.

'Radiography,' said Doctor Leapfrog, the radiographer.

'What's radiography?' asked Little Bear.

'Radiography is when Little Tiger goes into this box and we shine a light behind him. The light will shine through him, and standing there in front of him I shall be able to look *right through* Little Tiger and see what's wrong with him!' said Doctor Leapfrog. 'Aha!' he cried. 'One of his stripes has slipped!'

So now we know what was wrong with Little Tiger. One of his stripes had slipped!

'That's nothing serious,' said Doctor Leapfrog. 'Just a little operation, and Tiger will be better.'

'What's an operation?' asked Little Bear.

'An operation is when Little Tiger gets an injection to make him feel good, and then he goes to sleep and has a lovely dream. When he wakes up, the operation is all over, and Tiger will be better.'

But the fox was going to have a little
operation first.

'Injections are no fun for small animals
like you!' said the fox, showing off. 'You
need to be big and brave to have injections.
They prick!'

'They prick, do they?' said Little Bear.
'Oh, that won't bother us, Mr Fox!

A tiger is a tiger, you know, and a bear is a
bear.'

The fox had a little injection, and a
lovely dream, and then the operation was
all over, he hadn't noticed anything, and
his paw was better.

Then it was Little Tiger's turn.
He had a little injection to make him
feel good, and a lovely dream, and then
the operation was all over, he hadn't
noticed anything, and Tiger was better.

'You can go home the day after
tomorrow, Mr Tiger,' said Doctor
Bullfrog. 'You are totally, completely
cured! Now then, just you have a good
night's sleep!'

Tiger had lots and lots of visitors next day.

Auntie Goose brought him a bottle of gooseberry cordial. 'And when you're home I'll bake some cakes,' she said.

'With cream filling and almond icing?' asked Little Tiger, getting a kind of homesick feeling in his mouth.

The yellow duck with the harmonica played him a waltz tune, and the hare with the soft paddy paws brought him two mushrooms he had picked in the woods.

And when they went to sleep that
night, Little Bear said, 'I'll cook your
favourite food when we get home, Tiger.'

'Oh yes!' said Tiger. 'I know what I
want you to . . .'

But at that point he fell asleep.

Next day all their friends came to take
Tiger home.

In a band.

'How much farther is there to go?'
asked Little Tiger, who was feeling very,
very homesick now.

'Almost exactly eight hundred metres,'
said the great big, kind grey elephant. 'As
the crow flies.'

'Now,' said Little Bear, when they were home, 'ask for your favourite food and I'll cook it.'

'River trout with almond sauce and breadcrumbs!' cried Little Tiger.

'Try something else,' said Little Bear.

'Egg noodles with almond sauce and breadcrumbs!' said Little Tiger.

'Try another something else,' said Little Bear. 'Say *soup*, do say *soup*!'

'Oh yes!' cried Little Tiger. '*That's* what I was going to say!'

And so they had soup. Soup with a few shiny little beads of fat floating on top, made with parsley in it, and carrots from the garden.

'But next year,' said Little Bear, 'it will be *my* turn to be ill, and *you* can make me better, all right?'

'Naturally!' said Little Tiger. 'Of course!'

So then they went to sleep, and they slept all night until next day.